On the
Rocks

On the Rocks

Eric Walters

ORCA BOOK PUBLISHERS

Library and Archives Canada Cataloguing in Publication

Title: On the rocks / Eric Walters.
Names: Walters, Eric, 1957– author.
Series: Orca currents.
Description: Series statement: Orca currents

Identifiers: Canadiana (print) 20190169036 | Canadiana (ebook) 20190169044 |
ISBN 9781459823648 (softcover) | ISBN 9781459823655 (PDF) |
ISBN 9781459823662 (EPUB)

Classification: LCC PS8595.A598 O58 2020 | DDC jc813/.54—dc23

Library of Congress Control Number: 2019943989
Simultaneously published in Canada and the United States in 2020

Summary: In this high-interest novel for middle readers,
fourteen-year-old Dylan, sent to live on a remote island with
his estranged grandfather, discovers a stranded orca.

*Orca Book Publishers is committed to reducing the consumption of
nonrenewable resources in the making of our books. We make
every effort to use materials that support a sustainable future.*

Orca Book Publishers gratefully acknowledges the support for its publishing
programs provided by the following agencies: the Government of Canada,
the Canada Council for the Arts and the Province of British Columbia
through the BC Arts Council and the Book Publishing Tax Credit.

Edited by Tanya Trafford
Design by Ella Collier
Cover artwork by stocksy.com/Zoran Djekic
Author photo by Sofia Kinachtchouk

ORCA BOOK PUBLISHERS
orcabook.com

Printed and bound in Canada.

23 22 21 20 • 4 3 2 1

*To those who dedicate their lives
to caring for animals in need.*

Chapter One

My stomach rose up as the boat slammed down through another wave. I hung on to the railing—and leaned slightly over the side just in case. The spray showered me. I was already soaked to the bone, so it really didn't matter. I couldn't get any wetter unless I fell into the ocean. That thought made me hang on even tighter as my mind started to play with the idea of being tossed overboard. The crew might not even notice that I was in the water. Then they'd have to turn around and try to find me before I disappeared under the waves.

"How are you doing?"

I turned around. It one of the crew members. He had told me his name was Jag Singh. He was wearing an orange rain suit with reflective stripes and a matching orange turban without reflective stripes.

"I've been better," I answered.

"It could be worse out here."

"I'm not sure how it could be worse than this."

"Oh, it can be, believe me. There have been trips where *I've* been hanging over the edge, sharing my lunch with the fish."

"I can't even think about food."

"Don't worry. It's only another twenty minutes until we dock."

I nodded and instantly regretted the motion.

"I'm sure you don't remember me," said Jag.

"You introduced yourself two hours ago," I replied.

He laughed. "No, I mean from a long time before that. You were only about five years old, so that would have been what, eight or nine years ago?"

"I guess. I'm fourteen now."

"Yeah, that sounds about right. You and your mother came over to the island. How is she anyway?"

"What?"

"Your mother. How is she doing?"

I gave him a curious look. What was it to him?

"She and I went to school together."

"Oh, I didn't know that," I said.

"She was always nice to me." He pointed up at his turban. "Sometimes other people weren't as nice."

"That sounds like her. She's nice to everybody." She'd always said that "people are people," and she treated everyone the same way.

Jag chuckled. "Good to know she hasn't changed. So how is she doing?"

For a split second I thought about telling him the truth—that my mom was in an alcohol-abuse treatment program—but what was the point? There would be no gain for her or for him or for me in telling him.

"She's fine. She's doing well."

"Great to hear that. Will she be joining you on the island?" he asked.

"Maybe later this summer. For now it's just me. I'm going to be here for six weeks." *Until my mom gets out of treatment*.

"It would be good to see her again to say hello and catch up."

"I'll tell her you said hi when I talk to her." What I didn't tell Jag was I didn't think Mom was even allowed to use her cell phone—at least, not until she was in better shape.

"Thanks. So how long has it been since you've seen your grandfather?" Jag asked.

"A long time." It was probably the time I'd been out here when I was five. I basically had no memory of him.

"You know he's a pretty famous painter, right? That must be where your mother got her talent."

My mom is super talented, but she hasn't painted much in the last few years. I know about my grandfather being a well-known painter but not much more about him—other than that he and Mom don't get along. That's why we never see him.

"I know some of your grandfather's paintings have sold for a lot of money," Jag said.

"Yeah, I heard that too," I said. "So how well do you know him?"

"Not really well, but we deliver his supplies—you know, groceries, things for the house, even his art supplies. We probably come out this way every three or four weeks. We ferry supplies and passengers to all the islands around here." He paused. "Not that your grandfather has a lot of visitors."

"But he does have some visitors?"

"Not many and not in a while. Sometimes his agent. I like him, but your grandfather can be a little…a little, um…"

"Hard to get along with?" I asked.

"Yeah, I guess so. He's probably friendliest to Captain Ken. He and Captain Fukushima go a long way back. But you know, those artsy types can be a little bit *different*."

My mother probably would have used other words to describe her father. Then again, what did I know? It wasn't like I'd heard her say much about him at all.

And really, even with the bad stuff, how much truth was there in anything she said? She was telling her side of things.

"There's the tip of the island now."

I looked up and through the spray and mist. Rocks and trees were visible in the distance. There were dark clouds behind that—it was beautiful and scary and eerie all at once. It looked like a painting, all serious and dark. Was it an omen of what was to come?

"I have to get to my station and prepare to dock," Jag said. He walked away.

We bounced along. We were getting closer, but not fast enough. I could just see the waves smashing against the rocks on the shore. There were lots of rocks and trees—tall, sweeping trees. The only tall things where I live are apartment and office buildings.

We rounded another little point, and the wind and the waves died down a bit. Up ahead I saw the outline of a small wooden pier jutting into the water. That had to be where we were heading. I *hoped* that was where we were heading. I just wanted to get solid ground under my feet again.

We entered a protected little cove. The wind and waves definitely were less powerful now, and there wasn't even any spray in my face. I almost missed the spray. It had been the only thing keeping me from throwing up again—not that I had anything left in my stomach to come up.

I could make out a figure on the dock. He was wearing a dark rain jacket, and his face was hidden under the hood. It had to be my grandfather— my mother's father. But that didn't make him any less of a stranger.

Closer and closer. The dock was made of heavy-looking beams, and the sides were rimmed with thick black tires.

The man—my grandfather—looked up and gave a little wave. Reluctantly I waved back. Then I turned and went inside to retrieve my bag.

Chapter Two

Jag tossed a rope to the dock—to my grandfather—and he grabbed it and pulled us in. The engine roared, and then we bounced against the tires. I held on to the rail to stop from tumbling over. Jag ran down the side of the boat and jumped onto the dock. He tied the back of the boat to the dock while my grandfather tied the front. I waited until the boat was snug against the dock and then climbed off the boat. The dock was wet and slick. I started to slip, then regained my footing.

"Hello, Dylan," said my grandfather. He held out his hand.

I studied him, looking for emotion. Was he happy to see me? No, he looked as nervous and uneasy as I felt.

"I guess you know who I am," he said.

"I've seen pictures, but you're older."

He laughed—it was a nervous laugh. "A lot older, but then, so are you."

Jag was holding a large crate.

"Let me give you a hand with that," my grandfather said. He turned and walked away from me. I felt relieved. I thought he was probably relieved too.

How was this going to work? How was I going to spend the next six weeks with a man who was my grandfather but basically a stranger? It probably would have been easier if he actually were just a stranger.

The way Jag and my grandfather were straining with the crate, I knew it had to be heavy. They set it down on the dock. My grandfather was old, but he looked pretty strong. He had gray hair and matching gray stubble but moved like somebody a lot younger.

"Do you have my art supplies in there?" he asked.

"I have a second one for you," Jag said.

Jag disappeared into the boat's cabin at the same time the captain stepped out.

"How are you doing, Angus?" the captain asked as he stepped onto the dock and extended his hand toward my grandfather.

"Well, my friend. And you?" The two men shook hands, and for the first time I saw my grandfather smile.

"Good, good, can't complain. So this is your grandson?" the captain said, gesturing to me.

My grandfather turned to face me. He seemed to be studying me. "That's what I've been told," he said, "but I don't think he looks much like me."

"You're right. He *doesn't* look like you," said the captain. "He's good-looking." He started laughing. So did my grandfather. "He does look like your daughter though."

I'd been told that before.

Jag came back carrying a second crate—it was smaller than the first.

"Jag, don't you think the boy looks like Becky?" asked the captain.

Becky. Nobody called her that these days. She was Rebecca or Rebe but never Becky.

Jag put down the crate and looked at me.

"I can see the resemblance. Especially in the eyes. There's something there. But I can also see that the weather is closing in."

"For sure," the captain said. "We better get going while we can or we're going to have to put in for the night here."

"You know you're always welcome," my grandfather said.

"Depending on how it goes once we're out there again, you might see us back for the night."

I thought it might be better if they did stay. They were basically strangers, but I felt more comfortable around Jag and Captain Fukushima than I did around my grandfather.

"Are you all right to get things up to your cabin?" Jag asked.

"We'll get them up," my grandfather said. "We'll manage."

They shook hands and said their goodbyes. As the captain shook hands with me, he pulled me in closer. "He's a good man," he whispered. "Even if he doesn't show it sometimes."

I nodded as he let go of my hand. I wasn't sure if his words were meant to be reassuring or a warning or both.

The captain and Jag got back on the boat. My grandfather helped them untie the lines and cast off. The engine roared as the boat backed away. It started to rain.

"No time to waste," my grandfather said. "Grab one end."

He took the front of the bigger crate, and I reached down and grabbed the other. We heaved it up. I was surprised by how heavy it was. I felt the strain in my arms and back.

The way we were positioned meant I was looking directly at him across the length of the crate. I wanted to look away.

"Hold on," he said. He shifted his grip and turned around so his back was to me and he could walk forward.

He started to walk, and I jerked forward along with him.

We stepped off the dock and immediately started up a steep path. It was very rough, with rocky steps and lots of places to trip. I almost lost my footing a couple of times. The rain was picking up and pelting against my face—it was cold and sharp and strong. The higher we got, the more the wind picked up.

I felt the weight in my arms and also on my back. I wasn't carrying only the crate—my pack was on my back. It contained basically everything I owned. My clothes—the few things I had—an extra pair of shoes, an old photo album and a couple of things I'd made for my mother for Mother's Day over the years. Everything else had either been left behind or sold out from under me, hocked to pay the rent or—well, sold.

Struggling up this hill might have been the first time I was grateful for not having much of anything.

"It's not much farther," my grandfather said, without looking back.

"I know. It's just through those trees, right?"

"Yeah." He turned around slightly. "You remember?"

I nodded. Walking up this hill had brought back memories—or at least a hint of memories. It was like I couldn't remember the path in my head but felt it in my legs. I'd climbed these steps. I'd walked this path before.

We got to the shelter of the trees. It didn't stop the rain, but it did break the wind. I looked past my grandfather and down the path. There was the cabin.

It didn't look very big. I'd figured it was going to be small, but it was smaller than I remembered it.

"Watch yourself," said my grandfather as we made our way up the wooden steps to the cabin.

"What?"

Before he could answer I tripped, almost dropping the crate.

I looked down. The middle stair was missing a board. My grandfather didn't miss a beat, and we continued up the steps and onto the porch. Finally we were under shelter.

"Put it down right here," he said. My back and legs were happy when we set it down. "You go inside, and I'll go down and get the other one."

"I can go," I volunteered without thinking.

He shook his head. "You've already carried more than your share. Besides, you're not dressed for the weather. Go inside and get changed into something dry."

He turned and set off. I watched him walk away. I stood there, the rain pounding down on the porch roof. A little bit of rain was being blown by the wind and misting over me. The door was right there. Somehow it seemed wrong to just walk in. But it seemed even more wrong to stand out here.

I hesitated. I almost knocked. That would have been beyond stupid. I partially opened the door and peered inside. Warm air flowed out. I let the door open completely. It was darker inside, but I could see old furniture— big, overstuffed furniture—and carpets on the floor. I smelled smoke, and then I saw where it was coming from—there was a big woodstove in the back. A fire was glowing.

I went to step inside and then decided I'd do one thing first. I grabbed the crate and hefted it up. I strained and struggled but managed to bring it inside, dropping it onto the floor.

I closed the door, and the sound of the rain was blocked out. Now I could hear a ticking clock and the crackling of the fire. I slipped off my pack and put it on top of the crate. It felt good to be free of the weight.

I looked around. The walls were covered with art. Some pieces were formally framed, but others were just canvas stretched over a wooden frame. Most of the paintings were of landscapes and animals of the area—killer whales, bears and otters. I knew they were my grandfather's. I recognized the style. I'd seen much more of his art than I had of him, and, like Jag said, he was pretty famous. At least, he was with those artsy types my mother used to hang around with when I was younger.

I couldn't help noticing that there were stacks of dirty cups and plates—some with half-eaten and moldy-looking food—on the counters and coffee table. It looked like he hadn't done the dishes for about a month.

A chill went through my body. I was wet and cold. I needed to get out of these clothes and into something dry. But I wasn't going to change in the middle of the room.

I walked over and pushed open a door. It was much darker in that room, but from the light coming in through a small window I could make out that it was a bedroom. There was a big, unmade bed in the middle and a cluttered dresser on the far wall. More cups and dishes too. This had to be my grandfather's room. I closed the door.

I went to the next one. I could smell what was in this room even before I pushed open the door—paint. My senses were confirmed. It was a studio. There were easels and drop cloths, big tables, containers of brushes—brush ends up— cans of paints, pallets and many, many more paintings.

Unlike every other room in the house, this one was tidy. Cluttered but tidy. No dirty dishes or moldy food.

Two of the exterior walls were actually floor-to-ceiling windows, and there were three skylights overhead, although they were partially covered in leaves and pine needles. Despite that, despite the clouds in the sky and the rain pounding down, there was still what my mother called "good light." I could see her being happy in here. I guessed my grandfather must be too. I knew that for a painter, this room would be as much their place as their bedroom. I backed out and closed the door on this room too. There was only one door left to check.

I tried to open it. It didn't budge. Was it locked? I put my shoulder against it and pushed, and it opened with some resistance. The bottom of the door was rubbing against the floor. Either the door had sagged or the floor had risen.

I peeked inside. I couldn't see much. The window in this room was even smaller than the one in the first bedroom. The interior was dark, and it had a musty smell. I wondered how long it had been since this door had been opened. I opened it wider and then fumbled along the wall, feeling for a light switch. I found it and flicked it, and a dim blue light came to life on the ceiling.

Another bedroom. In one corner was a big bed with a brass headboard and footboard. It was covered in pillows, and a few stuffed animals had been tucked into bed. There were pictures on the walls. More paintings, but they weren't my grandfather's. I recognized the style. These were my mother's. The ones she'd done at home had long been sold or traded. But these were definitely hers too. This had to be her bedroom from when she was little.

I heard the front door open. I felt like I'd been caught doing something bad. I turned to leave, but there was no way I could get out of the room without being seen. My grandfather was standing there in his rain jacket, still holding the smaller crate, staring right at me. I had to say something.

"I was looking for a place to change," I explained. "I wasn't snooping."

I turned the light off and with both hands pulled the door almost completely shut again.

"That's the room you're going to be using." He paused. "That was your mother's room."

I nodded.

"Your grandmother always kept it just the way your mother left it when she went off to art school."

That had to be twenty years ago.

"And then when your grandmother passed…well…"

She had died not long after my mother and I had last visited. I didn't really remember her. I did have one fuzzy memory of her pushing me in a wheelbarrow. That was it, and I wasn't even sure that was real.

"I need to get changed," I said. "Should I use the bathroom?"

"Only if you want to get wetter."

"What?"

"The outhouse is out the back and down the path. You'd best use your mother's room."

"Sure…okay."

I took a step toward the room and remembered that I didn't have my pack. My grandfather was standing right beside it. I walked toward him, and I could tell by his expression that he was thrown a bit.

"My bag," I said, pointing to it.

"Oh, yeah."

I grabbed the pack, spun around and headed back toward the bedroom. I put my shoulder against the door and opened it again. I turned and muscled the door closed, throwing the room into darkness. I turned on the light.

I took off my jacket. It was soaking wet. I looked around for a place to put it. I settled on one of the posts on the footboard. I opened up the pack. I wanted to get clothes out before I took clothes off. I could even put them away.

I walked over to the dresser. On top of it sat a framed picture of my mother.

She was younger—in her early teens. She was smiling. It seemed like a long time since I'd seen her smile, even before she'd gone away.

I wondered how old she was in that picture. I wondered why she looked so happy. Maybe back then she had lots of reasons to be happy.

I pulled open the bottom drawer. It was full of clothes. Underwear and stuff. I felt a rush of embarrassment. I pushed it closed. I opened up the next one. It had shirts and socks. And then the one above that. It held sweaters. Why was it full of clothes? Were these all my mother's clothes? It didn't matter. Either they were or they weren't, and it wasn't like I could pull them out and put my stuff in there instead.

I tried to push the drawers closed, and the top one jammed. Then one of the handles snapped off in my hand. I put it on the top of the dresser. Somehow I'd broken it. I hadn't really done anything, but I was sure I'd be blamed. I'd have to fix it before my grandfather noticed, but I couldn't do it now.

I noticed a closet door. Maybe I could hang up my shirts and this pair of pants in there. That would let the wet stuff dry. I pulled it open and saw that it was filled with clothes too. Stuffed full. Dresses and shirts and skirts and sweaters and lots and lots and lots of shoes. My mother loved shoes. I guess she always had. The floor was covered in shoes, and the clothes rod was so jammed that I didn't see how I could hang up anything. Putting my clothes away wasn't going to work now, but I still needed to change.

I started to take off my shirt. It was stuck to my body, and I had to peel it off. I kicked off my shoes, and my socks squished against the floor. I went to pull off my pants. My phone! I pushed my hand into my pocket. The pocket was soaked, and so was my phone!

I'd turned it off on the boat when we'd lost service, to save power, and then had put it in my pocket to protect it from the elements. Like that had worked. I turned it on. It slowly started to come to life.

"Come on, come on," I muttered.

The screen had a bluish glow, and then all the icons appeared. It was working. I noticed there was no cell service. I couldn't call or text or do anything that would tell me the phone was working for sure, but it did look like it was working. I just wished I had put it someplace waterproof. I really wished I still had my other phone—my good phone. The one my mother had pawned. I had a rush of anger just thinking about that.

I put the phone on the dresser and kicked off my pants. They were soaked, but at least my boxers were dry. I should have stuffed the phone in my shorts. Maybe it wouldn't have gotten wet.

I looked up and saw myself reflected in the mirror above the dresser. I studied my reflection. My hair was wet and slicked back. It was too long. I needed a cut. I doubted that was going to happen over here, so I imagined it was going to get a lot longer.

My ribs were visible. My mother had always said I was too skinny and that I needed to eat more. I'd have been happy to if there had been more food in our place. I also figured I looked thinner than I was because I was so tall. Tall like my mother. Tall like my father—at least, my mother had told me he was tall. And, I knew now, tall like my grandfather.

I looked again at the picture of my mother on the dresser and then compared it to my reflection. I looked back and forth and then moved closer so I could see her image more clearly. I did look like her. My nose and eyes. The difference was around the mouth. She was smiling. She used to smile a lot, even when there really wasn't a reason to smile. Me, I tended to scowl or smirk. In fact, smirking was the closest I could come to smiling most of the time.

I suddenly became aware that I was standing in my boxers in my mother's old bedroom. It didn't matter, but I still felt exposed. I pulled some clothes out of my bag and put them on. It felt good to be dressed and dry.

Now what? I could stand here or go out—to him. I didn't really want to do that, but what choice did I have? I couldn't just hide in here for the next six weeks.

Chapter Three

I finally worked up the nerve to leave the
bedroom. My grandfather was sitting at
the table. He didn't seem to notice me.
He had a pad and was sketching with
a piece of charcoal. I looked over his
shoulder at his drawing. It was a scene
of an otter sliding down a muddy bank.
It was very good—but why wouldn't
it be? He was a famous artist. He still

hadn't noticed me standing there. I figured I could ignore him too.

I pulled out my phone—still no signal. I walked over to the window. There had to be a signal there. Nothing. I might have to get out of the house or higher up or closer to the shore to find a signal.

"I'm going out," I said.

He didn't answer. I didn't think he had heard me. Fine.

I noticed his rain jacket hanging on a peg by the door. There was a second one—bright red—right beside it. I grabbed that one.

I pulled it on. It was a bit tight, but at least it would keep me dry.

I looked back at my grandfather. He still had his head down, sketching. I thought of saying something, but that would defeat my plan to ignore him. I went out onto the porch and closed the door behind me.

It was still raining but not as hard. As I stepped off the porch, I almost tumbled to the bottom. I'd forgotten about the missing board.

I followed a path that ran along the side of the cabin and then up the slope. Going uphill might be better for cell service, but this was also the way to the outhouse. An outhouse! Had I traveled back in time?

I saw a little building just up the path, but it looked too big to be the outhouse. The door wasn't completely closed. I could see it had a busted hinge. I grabbed the door with both hands, lifted and opened it up. This was a toolshed. There were lots of tools—shovels, spades, saws and hammers. A stack of wood stood in the corner. I pushed the door closed again—at least, as closed as I could get it with the broken hinge.

Through the trees I saw another little building. That had to be the toilet.

I pulled out my phone as I walked, shielding it from the rain.

"Come on, give me some bars."

There were none. No service.

I decided I'd use the toilet and then go back inside and finish unpacking. And then I thought of something I could do first. I stopped by the toolshed on the way back to the cabin.

I snugged the board into place. It fit perfectly. The nails and hammer I had grabbed from the shed had seen better days, but they would get the job done. I hammered the first nail in with two hits and then banged it two more times to make sure it was really down flat. I put a nail in the other end. Three hits this time. I pushed against it. It felt solid, but I was going to add two more at each end just to be safe.

"What are you doing?"

My grandfather was standing at the open door. He didn't look happy.

"I'm fixing the broken step."

"Oh…yeah…I was going to do that, but you know what they say. 'There's always time tomorrow.'"

I almost gasped. "What?"

"'There's always time tomorrow.' My father used to say that," he said.

My mother always said it too.

"Your grandmother used to trip on that step all the time."

"But she's been…gone…for a long time."

"Nine years next month."

"This step has been broken for *nine years*?"

"Closer to eleven. I guess sometimes there isn't a tomorrow for steps." He paused. "Or for people."

He looked like he was going to say something else, but he didn't. Instead he turned and went back inside.

I was going to hammer in the remaining nails, but it started to rain harder again. I stood up and tested the stair with my weight. There was a little give, but that was probably because the beams underneath were a little soft. A wooden porch in a rainforest was going to rot eventually no matter how well it was built.

I went inside. My grandfather was back at the table, but he wasn't working yet. I laid the tools down on the floor.

"The jacket," he said.

"Yeah, it was by the door—I just put it on."

"I put it out there for you, I hoped it would fit. It belonged to your grandmother."

I removed the jacket. "It's a little tight, but it worked." I hung it back up on the peg.

I turned around. My grandfather was looking at me. I pulled out my cell phone so I could avoid a staring contest.

"That won't work," my grandfather said.

He was still looking directly at me.

"You won't be able to get a signal here."

"Yeah, I can't seem to get a signal anywhere in the house."

"You won't get a signal anywhere on this side of the island."

"*What?*"

"There's no reception on this side of the island."

"But…but…how is that possible?"

"There are no cell-phone towers. I'm glad too. Those things are a blight on the landscape. There are some on the far side, where there are some year-round houses and cabins."

"So you don't have a cell phone?" I really *had* gone back in time!

He laughed. "I wouldn't have one even if it did work out here."

"But you do have email, right?"

He laughed. "Do you really think I have that internet thing out here?"

"But how do you communicate?"

"I have a shortwave radio. I call in to the harbor when I need groceries and supplies. It works."

I was going to say something more about cell phones, but then I thought of something else.

"Do you have a TV?"

"Nope. Same as the phones. No signal. Didn't those people tell you any of this?"

I shook my head. "They just told me I had a choice of coming here or, well, a foster home."

"I guess this is better than that then."

I almost said "Not much" or "At least they'd have a TV" but thought better of it.

"Looks like we're stuck with each other for a while, kid. Maybe we should have supper and talk about the elephant in the room," he said.

What elephant? "I don't know what that means," I said.

"It means we should talk about why you're here. About your mother and about your mother and me. Does that seem right?"

I nodded. Finally I was going to get some answers.

Chapter Four

So far we'd done the eating part of the meal but not the talking part. I got the feeling that neither of us knew where to start. I was hungry, and the baked beans had tasted very good. I'd already gotten a second helping.

"Not fancy," my grandfather said. "I'm an artist, not a chef."

"It's warm and there's lots of it, so I'm good."

"I know your mother doesn't have a very good impression of me."

I hadn't expected him to be so blunt. I nodded.

"You have to remember that there are two sides to every story."

I had a feeling I was about to hear his side.

"And people with drinking problems, well, they can't always be trusted to tell the truth," he continued.

I wanted to defend her, to yell at him, but I knew what he was saying was true.

"She probably told you that I'm anti-social and that I don't get along with people."

I nodded again.

"Well, at least we agree on that. I *am* hard to live with. I'm stubborn to the point of stupid sometimes."

The bluntness continued.

"But the troubles with your mom... well, they all started with that, with that...*man*," he said with a sneer.

Wait. The words were sinking in. "You mean my father?"

"Yes. I told her not to get involved with him. We tried to warn her, but she never saw anything bad in anybody."

"And she told me that you never see anything but bad in people," I blurted out.

He smirked. "Do you know just how talented your mother was?"

"She was good, sure."

"She could have been great! She could have been better than me, but she threw it all away," he said. "In the end, your art is all that matters—that's all that remains when you're gone. And she betrayed it."

"The way you betrayed your daughter and your grandson?"

He didn't answer.

"Do you have any idea what my life has been like?" I asked. I felt the anger bubbling up.

"Of course not. How could I?"

"You would know if you hadn't turned your back on us!" I yelled.

"It wasn't me who turned my back on you."

"Wasn't it? I guess I didn't notice you standing there offering to help when there wasn't any food in our apartment or when we got evicted or when my mother practically drank herself into a coma!"

"And if I *was* there, would it really have helped?" he asked.

"Would it have hurt?" I asked. "Could it have been any worse?"

"I can't change the past, but I'm pretty good at reading the future. In the end, people disappoint you."

I'd had enough. I got up from the table. "Well, I'm sorry in advance for disappointing you."

"I didn't mean that."

"I don't care what you meant. I just want to know one thing. Why did you even agree to let me come here? Why did you even bother?"

"The social workers contacted me. I didn't know if I could do anything for you, but I had to try. You should show some gratitude."

"Yeah, thanks for everything you've done for me my entire life."

"It could be worse. You could be in a foster home right now."

"I could, but that doesn't mean it could be worse. Maybe I should go find out."

"Maybe you should." My grandfather looked hard at me and then started eating again. Clearly he was done talking.

I stomped away from the table and straight toward my mother's room. *My* room. I pushed the door shut. If the stupid door wasn't so swollen, I would have slammed it.

Chapter Five

It had been five nights and five days of almost exactly the same thing. My grandfather stayed up late to work, and I got up early to eat and get out of the cabin. I'd spent as much time as I could wandering around the island. I had walked for about an hour along the beach, until I came up to some rocks forming a cliff that blocked my way.

The next day I had walked twice as far in the other direction before I turned around. I figured if I stayed close to the shore, there was no way I could get lost.

Also, by sticking to the shoreline I thought I was less likely to run into any bears or wolves or cougars. I assumed from my grandfather's paintings that all those creatures lived here on the island.

As long as it wasn't raining, it wasn't bad being outside. When it was raining, I spent time in my room, on the porch and even in the shed. In my mind, my grandfather and I were having an unofficial contest to see who could say the fewest words to the other. One day I said twenty-one words to him. He'd said twenty-three. So I won.

When I closed the bedroom door now, it glided shut and just kissed the frame. It was as smooth as silk. On my second day here, I'd oiled and adjusted the hinges and used a plane to shave the bottom and side.

Along with ignoring my grandfather, I'd tried to do things around the place to earn my keep. I was going to eat his food—what choice did I have? We were stuck with each other. But I wasn't going to take his charity. I'd fixed the hinge on the toolshed door so it closed properly too. Then I'd cleaned out the shed and organized it. I'd even fixed the handle on the dresser in my room. Maybe I'd broken it, but I'd also fixed it. That last one was sort of a draw.

I took the red rain jacket from the peg beside the cabin door and slipped on my boots. I went down the steps—all of them. It felt good knowing I'd replaced the missing one. I thought it would have made my grandmother happy. That thought made me happy.

Spending so much time by myself had given me time to think. I'd thought about my mother in treatment. I'd thought about what it must have been like growing up here. I'd thought about my grandmother. I'd thought about my grandfather. I doubted he'd been thinking about me. All he did was paint. Mostly in his studio, but sometimes he took his paints and easel and worked outside. We'd bumped into each other a couple of times this week—he was painting, and I was walking on the beach. It's harder to ignore somebody when you see them by accident. Today, though, there would be no danger of us running into each other.

The yellow kayak was pulled up from the beach where I'd left it. When I'd cleaned out the shed, I'd found two kayaks in the rafters. I'd taken them down and cleaned up the one that looked to be in the best shape. If there was any reason it wouldn't float, I couldn't see it. I could have asked my grandfather, but that would have meant speaking to him. I'd also found a life jacket and a double-bladed paddle that I knew kayakers used because I'd seen them on TV before.

I picked up the kayak and brought it to the water's edge, putting it back down so it was barely on the beach and mostly in the water. There wasn't much wind, and the waves were small. Much smaller than they'd been the last couple of days. I figured today might be my best opportunity to get out on the water. I put on a life jacket and carefully stepped into the kayak. It wiggled, and I thought it was going to tip, but it didn't. I settled into the seat, tucking my legs into the front. With the paddle I pushed against the ground. I moved a little and a little more and then popped free and skittered out into the water.

The waves bounced me around and tried to push me back to shore. I dug in my blades and paddled out and away—left, right, left, right, left, right. I was pleasantly surprised at how fast and how far I was going. Either this was really easy or I was a fast learner.

I kept paddling and riding over the waves. I had the strange sensation that I wasn't so much going through the water as hovering over it. A big wave hit directly in front of me. The nose of the kayak dipped slightly, and a shower of spray hit me directly in the face. But I was feeling more confident. The waves weren't going to topple me. I could ride them out, almost ride above them.

I paddled around and started enjoying myself. I found that by paddling on only one side I could easily change directions, even make the kayak go in a tight little circle. I soon discovered that it was better to head directly into the waves than have them hit me on the side. Riding the waves up and down—which was a little scary at first—was actually fun.

Now I had to make a decision. I could stay here in the little cove, or I could go out a bit farther and follow the shoreline. I could, technically, circle the entire island. Okay, that made no sense, but I decided to keep paddling a little bit farther. I headed straight out toward the open water.

I focused on paddling. Glancing left and right, I realized I'd already passed the rocks that marked the sides of the cove. I wasn't in the cove anymore. I was in the open ocean. The wind had picked up, but strangely the waves seemed to have settled down. The water was flatter, the bumps fewer, and the ride was smoother.

Now I had to decide which direction to go. To the left was the beach. I'd previously walked pretty far in that direction. To the right were the rocks that had blocked me from exploring. That was the way I wanted to go. I had to see what was on the other side of those rocks.

I dug in harder to the left and quickly turned in the other direction. To my right was the island. To the left, as far as I could see, was nothing but ocean. No, wait. In the distance a thin line and a few bumps were visible through the gray. Mountains on the mainland. That was the direction of civilization, the way off the island. If I spun in that direction and paddled all day, I could probably get there.

What a strange thought. What a *wrong* thought. What I could probably do was drown or get lost. So instead, I paddled to put myself closer to the island shore.

I got back into the rhythm of paddling. All I had to think about was left, right, left, right. I focused on putting the paddle blade in the water just the right way. There was something almost hypnotic and calming about it.

Until I saw the fin burst out of the water directly in front of me.

Chapter Six

It was big and black, and it appeared and then was gone.

I stopped paddling. I bobbed on the waves, afraid to move or splash or breathe. I scanned the water. There was nothing but water. I must have imagined it. If it was a shark, it was the size of a submarine. And I was sitting in a thin piece of fiberglass.

The fin reappeared. It looked a lot smaller and, thank goodness, was moving away. It disappeared under the water again. Should I just wait until it left, or should I spin around and paddle like crazy in the other direction? Before I could decide, another fin broke through the surface near me, and then another and another! They were much closer now, between me and the shore. They came up out of the water and then disappeared beneath again.

My brain raced, trying to make sense through the fear. Not sharks. Sharks didn't travel together. And then I remembered that a shark's dorsal fin has a straight edge. A dolphin's curves toward its tail. These were dolphins. It was a bunch...um, a herd...no, that was wrong. Dolphins were like fish, so it must be a school. I was seeing a school of dolphins.

Just then a gigantic fin rose very close to my kayak. Below it I saw a black back and a flash of white and then a head. It wasn't a dolphin—it was a killer whale, and it was looking right at me! It slid back under the water, and a second one breached right beside it. It was enormous—or was it just closer to me than the last one? There was a loud sound, like breathing, and I spun around. There was another one on the other side of my kayak. I was in the middle of them.

I sat there, stunned and shocked and scared. The fins kept popping up and out of the water on both sides of me and then in front of me. I bobbed along as they moved forward. Soon they were all in front of me. I tried to count them, but it was impossible as they moved in and out, up and down. Let's just say there were a lot of them. They were moving quickly, and I watched as they got smaller and farther away. Finally they disappeared.

My whole body shuddered. I took a deep breath. That had been amazing. Just amazing. I found myself wishing they would reappear and come back. But more than anything I wanted to get land under my feet. I started paddling back to the cove.

Left, right, left, right, I paddled. I kept glancing over my shoulder for dorsal fins that never appeared. I was disappointed. And relieved.

Some time later, back at the cabin, I was startled by the front door opening. I looked up from the table. My grandfather had an easel over his shoulder and a canvas in his other hand. I had thought he was quietly working away in his studio. He nodded his head slightly. I was going to add that to our word count for the day. I was now ahead one to nothing.

He leaned the easel against the wall, put down the canvas and removed his coat. Underneath was a white knit sweater that was stained with paint. The stains weren't new. He wore this sweater all the time.

He came over and looked at the books scattered in front of me. "You're interested in orcas?"

I could have just said "yep" and stayed four words ahead, but I didn't.

"I saw a school of them today. When I was kayaking."

I had just put him in the lead.

He nodded. "A group of whales is called a pod. You found the kayaks in the shed."

"Yeah, I cleaned one of them up."

"And you were out kayaking when you saw the pod?" he asked.

"They sort of surrounded me."

"Were there about ten of them?"

"I think so. It was hard to tell. Fins just kept popping up and then disappearing."

"Come and I'll show you something."

He walked toward his studio. I got up and followed. The door to his studio was sticking a bit too. Maybe the next time he went out, I'd try to fix it.

He was fumbling around, searching through a series of stacked canvases. He found one and pulled it out. The painting was a side view of six or seven dorsal fins. Two of the whales had their backs out of the water. In the background was the cove.

"Do you recognize any of them?" he asked.

How was I supposed to answer a question that stupid?

"It's not as stupid as it sounds," he said.

Had he read my expression?

"They have distinct dorsal fins. Do you see this one?" he asked, pointing at the painting. "He has a notch close to the bottom of his fin, and the white patch around his eye is—"

"I saw him!" I exclaimed. "He came up close to the surface and turned to look at me."

"I'm not surprised. He's the youngster in our resident pod."

"I don't know what that means," I said.

"We have a pod that lives around here. I can recognize them all. In the late summer, when the salmon are running, we often get a superpod, as other pods come for the feast."

"So this is a fish-eating pod instead of one that hunts and kills seals or other mammals."

"You know about orcas?"

"I know some," I said. What I knew was what I had just read.

I looked at the painting again. It was so realistic. So good.

"I did a series of paintings about this pod. But I haven't been out on the water for a while...years, in fact."

"I got the other kayak out of the rafters. I could clean it up and we could go out together," I said.

Judging from his expression, he seemed as surprised by what I'd said as I had been when the words came out of my mouth.

"I have to finish up a painting tomorrow."

"Sure," I said. Why did I think he would want to do anything with me?

"But how about if we go out the day after that?"

"Yeah, sure. I guess that's okay."

Chapter Seven

I set the red kayak down on the shore beside the yellow one. It had a couple of dings in the hull, and the paint was scraped off in more than one place. I'd really had to clean it out. It looked like some squirrels had been using it as a nest.

I made sure that both kayaks were well above the high-water line. The tide had just hit its high mark and was starting to recede. I'd learned the pattern. Twice a day. After high tide the water went down for six hours, and then it came back in over six hours till it got back to high tide. Two highs and two lows every day.

That morning my grandfather and I had had breakfast together. We'd talked. I hadn't even done a word count. We'd basically kept to safe topics. It turned out he knew a lot about whales. He knew a lot about all animals. He'd even shown me the canvas he was working on. I'd recognized the spot. It wasn't far from where I was standing right now. After that he'd set out to paint. He'd taken his paints, supplies, easel and the canvas he was working on and left while I finished up the dishes.

There were no more piles of dirty dishes around the cabin. I had tackled them in the first few days I was here. I liked order. There wasn't much I could control in my life, but at least I could control what was around me and keep a place tidy.

Now that the second kayak was down on the beach and ready for our adventure the next day, I planned to go back up to the cabin and clean out the gutters. They were filled with pine needles, leaves and branches and really needed to be cleaned. I couldn't say I was really looking forward to the job though. It had stormed badly the night before, and the water had poured down the side of the house because the gutters were so filled with garbage. They had to be cleared, but now that the sun was out, I started thinking that maybe they could wait for another day. I could let my grandfather know I'd gotten the kayak out. I wanted him to know. I also really wanted to go back out to see the killer whales, and I wanted somebody to go with me. I knew they wouldn't hurt me, but it was still scary to be out on the water alone with those gigantic creatures. It would be nice to have somebody else with me.

I strolled along the beach until I came to the rock cliff that had blocked my way when I had first started exploring. I'd discovered that at low tide I could get around them, but for now I had to head inland to go any farther. I climbed up a path and then onto the rocks. They were rugged and sharp, and I had to move carefully from rock to rock. When I reached the top of the cliff I could see the ocean again. Despite the sky being clear, the water looked dark and angry. It was like last night's storm had drained into the ocean.

I looked over the other side of the rocks and spotted my grandfather. He was on the beach. It looked like he was painting the rocks I was standing on. If I stood here long enough, I wondered, would I make it into the painting?

He waved, and I waved back. I started to make my way down to him. Toward the bottom the way got a bit more dangerous because the rocks were slick. The waves were really crashing onto them.

I made it down to the sand and had started to walk toward my grandfather when I heard something. At first I thought it was the wind, but there was no wind. Then I thought maybe it was the waves, but the sound was all wrong. It sounded almost human. Like somebody was crying. But as far as I knew, there was nobody on this side of the island except me and my grandfather.

I turned my head back and forth, trying to locate the source of the sound. It was coming from behind me. I went back toward the rocks. The sound was gone. It had to be the wind or waves or just my imagination. But then it started again.

It was louder and even sadder-sounding.
I climbed up the rocks, and then I saw
I'd been hearing. I could hardly believe
my eyes.

Chapter Eight

My grandfather and I stood together on the rocks directly above it. I was staring at it, but my brain was having trouble processing what I was seeing.

"It happens. Not often, but it happens," said my grandfather.

"But they're so smart! I read it—you told me. How does this happen?"

"The storm last night churned up sediment, maybe even shifted the ocean bottom. And then the tide went out."

The creature let out another cry, and my whole body shuddered. Below us was a killer whale. It was stranded on the rocks. There was still a little water being splashed on it when a big wave crashed in, but it was completely trapped. And it was only going to get worse. The tide was going out. It would be going out for another five hours.

"Even though I just saw some up close, I didn't really realize just how big killer whales are," I said.

"And this one isn't even full grown," said my grandfather.

"It isn't?"

"This is the teenage whale I was telling you about. And teenagers, regardless of the species, sometimes do stupid things. His inexperience is probably why he's on the rocks."

"How do you know it's the same one?"

"Do you see the notch on the bottom of his fin?"

"Yeah, I see it!" I remembered him telling me about that detail and seeing it in his painting.

"I have spent a lot of time observing these whales. This may sound strange, but when I'm painting it's like I'm not just putting the images on canvas but etching them into my brain."

"I don't think that's strange. My mother says things like that too."

"Does she?" My grandfather paused. "His name is Oreo."

"*Oreo*? What sort of a name is that for a whale?"

"It's sort of unofficial." He paused again. "I named them all."

The whale—Oreo—called out again. It got an answer. Out in the ocean the rest of the pod was swimming about. Dorsal fins kept breaking the surface just off the shore, and a couple of heads kept popping out of the water. My grandfather called it "periscoping."

Suddenly he started yelling. "Get out of here!"

I jumped.

"Go away!" He waved his arms around, as if directing the whales out to sea.

"Are you afraid another one is going to get stranded?" I asked.

"Yes. They're family. They can't help him, and they can't abandon him. But the tide is still going out. They're putting themselves at risk."

"So what happens now?" I asked.

"Nothing. We're as unable to do anything as they are."

"Shouldn't we call for help? Radio somebody?"

"We can call, but by the time help arrives, it will be too late."

"Too late...wait...do you mean it will...it will...*die*?"

"A whale can't be out of water for that long. It dries out. It gets sunburned."

"There has to be something we can do."

My grandfather didn't answer.

"So we're just going to stand here and watch it slowly die?" I couldn't believe it. "That seems cruel."

"It does. But that's the way the world works." He turned and started down the rocks. "C'mon. Let's go back to the cabin, and I'll radio it in."

I remembered how slick and sharp the rocks were. I wanted to yell out, "Be careful!" but I didn't.

I looked down at the whale. His name was Oreo. Somehow it made it

74

even worse to know he had a name. His dorsal fin was moving up and down slightly. I could see him breathing. It almost looked like he was shuddering. He had to be terrified. Alone, nobody to help him, no way out, things only getting worse by the minute. I knew what that felt like. He cried out again, and I turned away. I ran to catch up to my grandfather.

Chapter Nine

My grandfather was on the radio. He had already called the coast guard. They had no ships in the area. He was speaking now with Captain Ken. I listened in on the conversation—I could hear both sides of it—and it didn't sound encouraging. Captain Ken wasn't close enough to help either, and they were talking about other boats that might be. He didn't have any other suggestions.

There had to be something we could do. If we'd had internet access, I could just google "stranded whale." I would have been sure to find some answers. Mr. Google always seemed to know things. Wait! We did have books!

I ran over to the table where I'd piled the books about whales that I'd been reading. There were four of them plus some old encyclopedias. There had to be something in them about stranded whales. I opened up the first book and started to scan. *No, I should use the index!* I flipped to the back and ran a finger down the listings. There it was—*stranded*. Pages 48–49. I flipped back and found the spread. I had started to read when a shadow fell across the pages. I looked up to see my grandfather standing over me.

"I'm reading about stranded whales and—"

I stopped talking when I realized he was holding a gun—a big gun.

"What are you doing...why do you have that?"

A tingle went through my whole body, because I was pretty sure I knew why.

"There's no help coming," he said. "It's like you said. We can't just stand there and watch him slowly die. That would be cruel."

"So...you're just going to kill him?"

"I don't have much choice. What else can we do? Is it right to leave him there to suffer when we know he's going to die?"

I didn't have an answer.

"I think it's better if you stay up here. There's no point in you seeing this."

I wanted to argue, but I *didn't* want to be there. I didn't want to be anywhere. I wondered if I'd hear the shot being fired.

My grandfather put a hand on my shoulder. "I'm sorry. I wish there was another way."

He let out a deep sigh and started for the door.

I couldn't even bring myself to watch him go. I heard the door open and close as my eyes fell back to the pages. And then they focused.

There was a picture of a pod of whales stranded on a beach. They weren't killer whales. The caption said they were pilot whales. The whales had been draped with sheets or towels or something. That had to be to protect them from the sun. And there were people carrying buckets, and one of them was dumping water onto the back of one of the whales. Isn't that what my grandfather had said—that they had to be protected from the sun and kept from drying out?

I jumped up from the table, still carrying the book, and ran out the door.

My grandfather was on the path, not far ahead.

"Wait!" I yelled.

He stopped and waited for me.

"These people are saving a herd, I mean a pod, of stranded whales," I said as I reached his side. I held the picture up for him to see. "They're stopping them from getting sunburned and drying out, the things you said would kill Oreo."

"Those are pilot whales," he said.

"But whales are whales. What difference does it make?"

"Those whales are on a beach. Not on sharp rock. There's no telling how much damage has already been done."

"We could look. We could get close enough to see."

"You have to know that when whales strand, it's often because something is wrong with them. They're sick and going to die anyway."

"Or maybe it's because they're inexperienced. You said it yourself. Teenagers do stupid things all the time," I said.

He didn't say anything for a while.

Finally he spoke. "We'd just be wasting our time."

"Do you have someplace you're supposed to be?"

"Of course not."

"So why not try? And even if we can't save him, we still wouldn't have wasted our time. We'd know we had done everything we could." I tapped my finger on the picture. "We have to try."

Again he didn't say anything. But he did look like he was thinking.

"Doesn't everybody deserve a second chance?" I asked. "Isn't it worth a try?"

"Probably," my grandfather agreed, nodding. "Besides, I don't think I could have done it."

"Done what?"

"Pulled the trigger. I don't think I could have done it. Let me have a look at that book."

Chapter Ten

I stood beside the whale. I'd never been this close to a living thing that was so big. He had reacted when I'd climbed down beside him, wiggling around. Now he had calmed down but was still trying to follow me with his eyes. I was taking my grandfather's advice and making sure I didn't get near the whale's mouth.

It was slightly open, and I could see the teeth. They were huge and sharp. I wondered if they looked like what a *T. rex*'s teeth would have.

I knew that killer whales had never harmed a person in the wild, but I'd read about a couple of people who had been killed by captive ones. This whale wasn't captive, but he was no longer free, and I didn't want to take a chance.

"Do you see much bleeding?" my grandfather yelled down. He was on the rocks above us.

"Just a little on the tail." Of course, I couldn't see the underbelly. I wondered if I'd even caused some damage when I came down and scared Oreo.

"I'm lowering the bin!" my grandfather called.

I stumbled a bit as I looked up at the blue container being lowered by a rope.

To steady myself, I put a hand on the whale. His skin felt like rubber—dry rubber. I quickly removed my hand and went to get the bin.

I put the bin on a flat spot. Inside it were sheets and towels. They were soaked in seawater and were cold and heavy. I pulled out the first sheet. It was a blue and green sheet from my grandfather's bed.

I spread the sheet out, starting at the whale's tail and pulling it toward the dorsal fin. The blood on the tail soaked into the sheet, making it blue and green and slightly reddish.

The whale cried out and shook a little bit. The feel of the sheet had to be terrifying. He opened and closed his mouth a couple of times. The teeth looked bigger than ever.

"It's okay," I said. "Don't worry... Oreo."

Calling him by name seemed to calm me. It seemed to calm Oreo as well, or maybe it was the sound of my voice. Anyway, I needed to keep talking.

"I'm going to put a second sheet on top of you," I said. "I need to protect you from the sun."

The sun was high in the sky now, and today of all days there was almost no cloud cover. It would have been so much better if it were raining.

I draped the second sheet over Oreo's dorsal fin and pressed it against his top and sides. Because the sheet was wet, it stuck nicely. The two sheets covered most of the whale. I used soaked towels to cover the rest of him, leaving the breathing hole on the top of his head open. I was also careful to avoid his mouth and eyes. I imagined it would be even scarier not to be able to see what was happening. The last thing this whale needed was to be more scared.

"You're doing a good job, Dylan," my grandfather called down. "Now you have to pour water over him!"

The sheets were wet, but they'd soon dry out in the sun. My grandfather had also told me about the dangers of the whale getting overheated. Pouring water would help to keep the whale cool, or at least cooler, as well as prevent him from drying out.

The bin was now empty. But it wasn't going to be for long.

The tide had continued to go out, and even the spray from the waves crashing up on the rocks wasn't reaching us anymore. What was left behind, though, was a large pool of water. I was going to use that pool.

I dipped the bin into the water and filled it to the halfway mark. Any more and it would be impossible to carry. As I picked it up, I realized it was already almost too heavy. I carried it over and tipped it, spilling the water over Oreo's back. It rained down the whale's side, pressing the sheets and towels even tighter against his skin.

"Does that feel better?" I asked.

Oreo answered by opening and closing his mouth and then blowing some air—and a little bit of water—through his blowhole.

"You have to keep moving!" my grandfather yelled. "You got him wet, but you need to get him cool."

I took the bin back down to the pool. I tried to figure out how much water was here. Was it enough, or would I eventually have to get water from the ocean? That could be a problem, as the tide was still going out and the rocks now rose higher from the beach. But I couldn't worry about that now.

I half-filled the bin again and lugged it back over the rocks. This time I went toward Oreo's tail. I poured it along his back and then onto his tail. Oreo flicked his tail, and some of the water was thrown back onto me.

This was what I'd have to keep doing—for hours and hours and hours.

Chapter Eleven

The sun was now directly overhead. I had stripped off my coat and my sweater and was still working up a sweat. Oreo didn't have a choice. I couldn't strip any layers off him. He needed more water to keep his temperature down. My arms were sore from the ten million bins of water I'd dumped over the past few hours.

I stopped and bent down right beside his head. I needed to rest, but I thought Oreo could use some reassurance. Maybe I was just imagining it, but I thought his eyes looked more calm when I was talking to him.

"I'm just taking a bit of a break," I explained. "You're doing well. The tide will be coming back in soon."

Soon meant in about an hour. But I'd still have to wait for high tide before there'd be any chance of Oreo getting free. As the sun got hotter and hotter, it was going to get harder and harder for me to get water. I'd pretty much used up all the water in the pool. Soon I'd have to climb down the rocks, dip the bin in the ocean and then muscle it back up, trying not to spill it or fall.

I was also getting very hungry. I hadn't eaten since breakfast, and even then I hadn't eaten much. My grandfather had gone off a while ago to get us both something to eat. I hoped he would be back soon. Not just because of the food—I wanted him here. I felt alone and a little scared.

Really, of course, I wasn't alone. And it wasn't just Oreo here with me. The entire pod was here, not far from the rocks, as close as they could come. Only the receding tide had forced them farther away. They still called out, and Oreo answered. He couldn't see them, but he knew they were there from their calls.

I jumped off the rocks and onto the sand. With the tide out, there was more beach now. Blue bin in hand, I walked toward the water. I came up to the stick my grandfather had stuck into the sand to mark the water level. The fact that it was now a dozen paces from the water confirmed that the tide was still going out.

My grandfather came around the other side of the rocks. Now that the tide was out so far, he could make it here along the beach. He had a pack on his back and something over his shoulder. As he came closer, I realized it was a green garden hose.

"Sorry it took me so long," he said. "But I got an idea."

"The hose."

"And this pump."

A bicycle air pump was attached to the end of the hose, held in place by gray duct tape.

"I want you to take one end of the hose up to Oreo. I'm going to try to pump water up from the ocean," he said.

"Do you think it'll work?"

"I'm a painter not a plumber, but it should work. At least, I hope it does."

"Not as much as I do. I was not looking forward to trying to lug this water up the cliff."

"Let's test it out. Take the end of the hose and the pack. There's food in there."

I dropped the bin to the sand, slipped on the pack and took the end of the hose. I uncoiled it in one direction. My grandfather unspooled it in the other as he headed for the water's edge. I climbed up the rocks. They were becoming less dangerous and less slippery as they dried.

By the time I reached Oreo's side, my grandfather was already standing in the ocean. I watched him pump the handle, up and down, up and down, up and down. He was working hard, but no water was coming out my end. It wasn't working.

But suddenly I heard a gurgling sound in the hose. It got louder and louder, and then water came squirting out.

I aimed the hose toward Oreo, and water ran down his back and over his dorsal fin. I screamed at the top of my lungs and waved one hand in the air, trying to get my grandfather's attention. My grandfather kept pumping, but he yelled back and gave a quick one-handed wave.

The water kept flowing, coming in little pulses. I ran it over Oreo's tail, along his back, on his sides and all the way to his head. This was incredible!

Oreo started to react. His big tail went up and down, his mouth opened to reveal his giant teeth, and he called out. It was a different cry. It sounded hopeful. Maybe he had reason to be hopeful. Maybe we both did.

Chapter Twelve

I slumped down against the rocks and finished off the last bit of my granola bar. I realized that Oreo was watching me eat. One eye was almost always looking at me.

"Sorry I couldn't share. You'll have to wait until you get back in the water. It won't be long now."

It wouldn't be long. I'd watched as the water got closer and closer to the marker. It was like a magic trick. Little by little, as the tide came in, the water crept up the beach. Finally the marker had been knocked over and washed away.

My grandfather had pumped up water every thirty minutes for the last five hours. He'd had to move several times as the beach disappeared under the rising water. Oreo was covered, wet and, I hoped, cool. I knew I was feeling cool. The sun had swung around, and now we were shaded by the rock overhang. I'd even had to put my sweater and jacket back on.

I stood up and looked out over the ocean. I caught sight of dorsal fins. This entire time the pod had stayed close. They seemed to be watching and waiting.

Just then there was a series of calls from the pod. Oreo replied. I figured the whales were checking in on him to make sure he was okay. Both sides sounded calm.

I wished that I could call out too. Not to my grandfather but to my mother. It would be so good to know she was doing okay. To let her know I was doing okay. To tell her all about today's adventure.

Somehow telling her would have made it all seem more real. It was strange that it didn't feel that way, when I'd been here doing this for the past nine hours. I was on these rocks, taking care of a stranded killer whale, and soon the tide would be back in and the whale would be free. He would rejoin his family, and everything would be all right again. At least, I hoped it would be. What if the tide didn't come in far enough, or the water wasn't high enough? Or what if Oreo was too injured to swim away? What then? I got to my feet. I couldn't allow myself to think that way. It was going to work. It had to.

"How are you doing?" my grandfather called down. He was above me again, on the top of the cliff.

"We're both doing fine."

My grandfather had stopped pumping water when there was no longer a safe place in the water for him to stand. The waves now pounded against the rocks, shooting spray up into the air.

"You're going to have to come up soon," he yelled down.

"I know."

I sat down right beside Oreo's head so we could look at each other. I was amazed that an animal this big had such a small eye. It wasn't much bigger than mine. And it didn't seem much different from mine either. There was a thoughtfulness in that eye—the whale was thinking. I was sure he knew I was trying to help, but did he think of me as a friend? No way to know for sure.

"Hey, Oreo, the next time I'm out there in the ocean in my kayak, I expect you to come up and say hello, okay? We're friends now. Actually, you're probably the only friend I have out here."

Oreo didn't answer, but I thought it looked like he understood.

"It's probably time to take off the covers," my grandfather yelled.

He was right. I started to peel away the sheet that covered Oreo's tail. I hesitated, wondering what I would find—had the bleeding stopped? I kept going. There was nothing underneath but black. Oreo lifted up his tail, almost like he was waving.

"It won't be long now," I said. "Soon that tail will push you through the water, back to your family."

I threw the sheet into the blue bin. I removed the second sheet and then the towels, one by one, until all of Oreo's body was revealed. His skin was slick and black, wet and shiny. I didn't know what his underside looked like. There might be cuts or scrapes or bruises, but what I could see of him looked good. As good as I could hope for.

Chapter Thirteen

My grandfather had already hauled up
the blue bin. The tide was coming in
quickly now. The waves were splashing
up and over Oreo's back and onto
the rocks behind him. It was making
the rocks slick, and I used the rope
that had lowered the bin to help steady
my climb. When I reached the rock lip,
my grandfather gave me a hand and

pulled me to the top. We stood there, gazing down on Oreo.

"He looks good," my grandfather said.

"I guess we'll soon find out. I wish there was something else we could do."

"You've done your part to keep him alive. It's up to the tide to do the rest."

As the tide got higher, the members of the pod got closer. For the past few minutes they'd been calling out almost continually. Oreo was answering back.

"It won't be much longer, will it?" I asked.

"Less than fifteen minutes, I'd say," replied my grandfather. "Each wave is washing up higher."

He was right. It was more than just waves washing over Oreo now. Some water remained after the waves went back out.

"I just need you to be prepared for whatever happens," he said.

"What do you mean?"

"We did everything we could. *You* did everything you could. You gave him a chance."

"More than a chance! We kept him covered and wet and cool the way we were supposed to."

"Yes, but whales are meant to float, not to be lying down on a hard surface. All that weight pressing down on the organs could have caused internal damage to the lungs or heart."

"He was breathing fine."

"And we can't tell how badly he's cut up on his belly. Those rocks are sharp. I just hope he doesn't try to escape before the water is high enough for him to swim free. That could lead to more damage."

I hadn't thought of that, but there really was nothing else we could do. If only I could tell him to wait—not that it would do any good. Oreo was being moved sideways by the waves now. His tail was going up and down, and it looked like he was moving slightly forward. Suddenly a gigantic wave crashed down, and Oreo popped off the rocks!

"Look at him go!" I yelled.

Oreo skimmed across the surface, heading out into the open ocean. Just the very tip of his dorsal fin was visible, and then he disappeared beneath the waves. He was heading straight toward the pod.

"There he is!" my grandfather called. "Do you see him?"

Many dorsal fins were visible, but I couldn't tell if one of them was Oreo's. Then I saw it—the one with the little notch. There he was!

"He's okay," my grandfather said.

"He's better than okay. He's with his family, and he's there because of us."

"He's there because of you."

"We both worked."

"You did more, but the work only mattered because you gave him a chance," my grandfather said. "He's back with his family because of you."

I let my grandfather's words sink in. I *had* given Oreo the chance. I had convinced my grandfather. And now Oreo was back with his family.

We stood there in silence and watched the whales. My grandfather reached out and placed an arm around my shoulders. I had to fight the urge to pull away. That had always been my first reaction. But this time I didn't. The weight of his arm felt warm and good and reassuring. Maybe I'd given myself a chance to be with family too.

Chapter Fourteen

"We better get going," my grandfather said.

"Let me just finish this up and sign off."

"Sometimes I regret getting this whole thing started."

I looked up from the computer. "You mean me?"

He snorted. "You're too smart to say something that stupid, Dylan."

I had to laugh. That was so like my grandfather—saying something nice but hiding it inside of something cranky so he didn't sound nice.

"What I mean is the whole computer, internet, cable TV, satellite thing," he said.

"Oh no, that's no mistake," I said. "It may have been the smartest thing you've ever done in your entire life."

I could have sworn I saw a small smile on my grandfather's face. Just for a second.

He had arranged a satellite connection to the world. Now we had internet. We had email. We could use the phone!

I'd been shocked when he first suggested it. He'd claimed it was to help him with "business," but I knew that wasn't the reason. He was doing it for me. It had taken almost two weeks for them get it installed out here, but life had been much more interesting over the ten days since then.

I got up and we headed for the dock. The path down was now a lot easier to manage. I'd smoothed out some bumps, removed some rocks and built a couple of little steps where they were needed. That was how I spent my days. My grandfather painted and I puttered—at least, when I wasn't on the computer or in the kayak.

"Do you think they'll be on time?"

"Captain Ken is pretty reliable that way."

We got to the dock. The two kayaks sat off to the side. I'd spent a lot of time in mine—and it *was* mine now. My grandfather had given it to me. Sometimes he paddled out with me, but mostly I was on my own. It didn't matter though. Sometimes I stopped being on my own once I got out there.

The salmon had started to run, so there was a superpod of killer whales around the island. Pretty much every time I went out, I caught sight of dorsal fins in the distance.

I'd seen Oreo and his pod a dozen times. I always took binoculars with me now, so even from a distance I could recognize him by the little notch in his dorsal fin. Most of the time the whales were so far away that I needed the binoculars. A couple of times they'd been closer, and once Oreo had come right up to me. It was a magical moment I will never forget.

As the rest of the pod had swum off, I'd spotted his dorsal fin coming toward me. I'd sat still as he swam around me, doing smaller and smaller circles. Finally he'd stopped, periscoped up, turned his head and looked at me. We'd locked eyes and stared at each other for a few seconds. Then he'd tilted his head, slipped back under the water and was gone, off to rejoin his pod. I'd watched the dorsal fin disappear and reappear as he surfaced for air.

It was pretty unbelievable. So much of what had happened over the last six weeks felt that way. My grandfather was still my grandfather. He could be lost for a day or two in his painting and hardly talk—or even eat, unless I brought him something. He could be moody and cranky, but he could also be kind and caring and nice. Most important, he was my grandfather. And I was his grandson.

"There it is!" I exclaimed.

The boat had rounded the point and was steaming toward us through the cove.

I scanned the deck but didn't see what I was hoping to see. I had an image in my head of how this was supposed to happen. She was going to be on the bow, waving to us as the boat came into view. I guessed she was inside—unless she wasn't on the boat at all. What if she'd changed her mind? What if she just couldn't do it? What if—and then I saw her. I recognized the brilliant red coat she loved, even though I couldn't really see the features of her face yet. It was the exact same color as the rain jacket I was wearing—her mother's jacket. That made me smile.

She waved, and I waved back. And so did my grandfather.

Jag came onto the deck. The boat got closer and approached the dock. Jag tossed a line, and my grandfather reeled the boat in. I expected Jag to jump off the end to secure the bow, but instead my mother did. She tied off the back expertly.

I ran down the dock to greet her. She stood up and gave me a big hug.

"It's so good to see you," I whispered in her ear.

"It's so good to *hug* you," she said. "Are you well?"

"I'm great. And you?"

"I'm doing really well too," she answered.

"Really?"

"Really. It's been hard, but I'm good. Honestly."

"I believe you." I took her by the hand and led her down the dock to where my grandfather was waiting. He looked nervous.

I think Jag and the captain realized this was a private moment. Neither of them had stepped off the boat yet.

I knew what I was going to say next because I'd practiced it—a lot.

"Mom, there's somebody I'd like you to meet. This is my grandfather, Angus. Grandpa, this is your daughter, Becky."

They both giggled nervously.

"I just thought you two should get to know each other."

"We know each other," she said.

"Not as well as you should," I replied.

"How was the ride out?" my grandfather asked, breaking the obvious tension.

My mom looked relieved. "It was good. It brought back so many wonderful memories. I see you still have the kayaks."

"Dylan got them out and cleaned them up."

"I'm out on the water all the time," I said.

"Maybe the two of us can go out. On the way in, we passed through a gigantic pod of killer whales just around the point."

I wondered if Oreo and his pod were among them.

"Maybe after I've settled in we could go out and find them," she said.

"That would be nice."

"If we're lucky," my mom continued, "maybe we could even get really, really close to them. It's pretty exciting to kayak right beside a whale."

"I can only imagine," I said.

My grandfather snickered.

We hadn't told her about what we'd done. She'd find out as soon as she got up to the cabin. My grandfather had painted the scene—Oreo on the rocks, covered with sheets and towels, and me standing over top of him, pouring water from the blue bin. In the background, in the ocean, were the dorsal fins of Oreo's pod. It was an amazing picture, and my grandfather was an amazing painter. Best of all was the title—*Family*.

"So would you like to tell my mother—your daughter—the surprise, or would you rather I did?" I asked.

"I think you should. After all, it was your idea," he said.

My mother looked concerned.

"Don't worry," I said. "Some surprises are good. Those boxes that are being unloaded from the boat don't contain just food and supplies. There are extra art supplies."

"We thought you could use your time here to sketch and paint...that is, if you want to," said my grandfather.

"That's...that's amazing...just amazing." My mom looked like she was going to cry.

"I made some space in my studio," he added.

"In your studio?" she asked. "But you hardly even let me in there when I was growing up!"

"You're grown up now...and I'm sorry for not letting you in. That wasn't right. Anyway, four weeks is a long time to be out here, and we want—*I* want you to be happy," my grandfather said. He looked nervous but pleased.

"Thank you. Thank you so much." She turned to me. "Are you sure you're okay about staying out here for another month?"

"I can't think of any place else I'd rather be."

We had all agreed that we were going to stay out here for the rest of the summer, until I had to go back and start school. That was the plan.

"How about you? Are you okay with it?" I asked my mom.

"This is my home," she said. "Some of the best times of my life were out here. It's good to get away from the city."

"It sure is," I agreed.

What my mom didn't know was that I had another plan I hadn't told anybody about yet. I'd done some research on homeschooling and the support I could get for my studies online. Just in case we decided to live here for the whole year.

"I know the last few weeks must have been tough for both of you," my mom said.

Grandpa and I exchanged a look. We both shrugged.

"We had our life-and-death moments, but I think we did pretty well," I said.

"We're a good team," my grandfather added.

My mom looked a bit confused. "Well, I guess we should get up to the cabin," she said.

"Maybe before we do that, you could start by giving each other a hello hug." I was determined to make these two important people in my life work things out.

They both looked uneasy.

"It's easy. Real easy," I said. "Both of you, come here."

I reached out and threw one arm around my mother and the other around my grandfather. I pulled them both in and felt them extend their arms around me and around each other.

"Grandpa, you were wrong about us being a good team."

"I was?" he asked.

"Yeah, we're not a team. We're a family."

Eric Walters, Member of the Order of Canada, began writing in 1993 as a way to get his fifth-grade students interested in reading and writing. He has since published more than a hundred novels and picture books. He is a tireless presenter, speaking to over 100,000 students per year in schools across the country. He lives in Guelph, Ontario.